I0681122

Tulsa!

The

Musical

by

David Gallagher

Synopsis, Plot and

Words to Songs

Tulsa! The

Musical

COPYRIGHT INFORMATION

Text and Conceptual Idea of the Musical Tulsa! Copyright © 15.3.2020 by The Author

Songs all Copyright © 2009 by The Author

The Author asserts legal and moral rights in accordance with the Copyright, Designs and Patent Act 1988, the principal legislation which governs UK copyright law covering intellectual property rights in the United Kingdom

The idea for the musical Tulsa! , the plot, text and these songs are the sole work of D. and the author relies on documentary evidence of included facsimiles of previous copywritten material to assert the superior moral and legal claim to material on similar themes written subsequently by other artists.

Front Cover and Jacket Designs

Copyright © The Author

2020

Printed on demand by

Lulu

All rights reserved No part of this publication may e reproduced, stored in a retrieval system, or transmitted, in any form or by any means, electronic, mechanical, photocopying, recording or otherwise, without the prior permission of the publishers.

This book is sold subject to the condition that it shall not, by way of trade or otherwise, be lent, re-sold, hired out or otherwise circulated without the publisher's prior consent in any form of binding or cover other than that in which it is published and without a similar condition including this condition being imposed on the subsequent purchaser.

ISBN: 978-1-67801-727-9

CONTENTS   PAGE

SYNOPSIS

TULSA! - THE MUSICAL COMPLETE VERSION IN FIVE ACTS

ACT 1 Scene I

Ormskirk Halloween 31 10 1992

Out with his jolly dentist, an old school acquaintance, D. meets J. who is a student at Edge Hill University working behind the bar. She is wearing a plastic raincoat with a sexy Halloween costume underneath, suspenders, black stockings, panties, bra, frilly things and wearing bright red lipstick. D. has been drinking many pints of beer with his dentist friend P. and it gives him the Dutch courage to go up to the bar and ask J. out. J. says "Sure" and D. does not even realise that she is from America because he is so amazed that she has said yes, because he is constantly rejected by all women.

Scene II

Tenerife

D. has already booked a holiday in Tenerife and it is for one person only. However, J. figures she can get a flight and so surprises him by turning up at the Hotel. They have a lovely holiday together, although on one evening D. drinks too much and is very ill. They have a show at the

Hotel and D. performs a song but it is not about J. because he has only just met her.

ACT II –Scene 1

Paris

Hard Rock Café

J. has friends near Paris so they go there visiting them and the Hard Rock Café. They go to the Palace of Versailles, Eiffel tower etc. The chorus perform all sorts of Rock songs appropriate to the year 1993 all of them written by D.

Act III - USA

TULSA

D. visits her family in Tulsa.

Scene IV - FRANCE

PARIS – HARD ROCK CAFÉ

FULL CAST AND CHORUS PERFORMING ROCK SONGS

Act V - USA

CHICAGO – RUNNING THROUGH AIRPORT FOR AGES TRYING TO BEAT THE SHUITTLE TO CATCH THE

PLANE WHICH THEY DO OUT OF BREATH- SINGING AND DANCING NUMBER – REPRISE I THOUGHT OF YOU SONG PIANO VOCALS

FULL CAST IN CHORUS SINGING ACCOMPANIMENT AND BACKGROUND DANCING

WASHINGTON

Scene I

Scene II – Cheltenham , England

ENGAGEMENT SCENE ST D.'s HOUSE HE PRODUCES THE ENGAGEMENT RING AND SHE SAYS YES – ENGAGEMENT

Scene III – Oklahoma State University

TULSA!   SETS

THE CRICKETERS ARMS, ORMSKIRK 1992
TULSA – J.'s PARENTS HOUSE WITH POOL
PARIS – HARD ROCK CAFÉ
CHICAGO AIRPORT
WASHINGTON - LINCOLN MEMORIAL
CHELTENHAM, ENGLAND
OKLAHOMA STATE UNIVERSITY

ACTION MAINLY 1992-1993
(1993-1995 still in love and writing songs about her after the split up)

AREAS ON THE STAGE
LIGHTING SHIFTS DEPENDING ON THE SCENE

AREA A: THE CRICKETERS ARMS PUB – GIRL BEHIND BAR – COUPLE OF MEN ON A SEAT.

AREA B: TULSA – SCENE BY THE POOL WITH J.'s FAMILY.(VERY FUNNY).

AREA C: HARD ROCK CAFÉ PARIS

AREA D: CHICAGO AIRPORT – RUNNING FOR A PLANE HAND IN HAND SINGING

AREA E: WASHINGTON – POLITICAL BUILDINGS SENATE WHITE HOUSE AREA

AREA F: CHELTENHAM

AREA G: OKLAHOMA STATE UNIVERSITY STUDENT ROOMS

CAST:

MAIN CHARACTERS : D. J.
FATHER MOTHER AND BROTHER OF J.
CHORUS at HARD ROCK CAFÉ AND DANCERS
CLOTHING: AS APPROPRIATE. J. DRESSED YOUNG LIKE AN EDGE HILL FOREIGN STUDENT ON A YEAR ABROAD AGED 20, D. AGED 30 AND WORKING IN INSURANCE.

PLOT

It is a love story. D. falls for J. when he meets her at a public house in Ormskirk. She is an overseas student doing film and media studies at Edge Hill University and D. works in the Claims Department for an Insurance Company. They have lovely holidays, fun, laughter and lots of music in Tulsa, Paris and Chicago, even just running through the airport, yes that is possible, and then Washington and Cheltenham (the races) and finally Oklahoma State University. At Oklahoma State University he goes out there to get a job so he can get a green card but she is in her final year and the idea of marriage is just too early or too much for her and so she rejects him by going off to Dallas with a married man for a day out. In the meantime D. borrows her old banger car that needs oil putting in every day and is leaking. He of course breaks down coming back from an interview for an Insurance sales job in the US with a US Insurer. He has secured two job offers but he cannot get a visa without marrying her and they are just engaged. D. returns home and feels so cold in the winter and frozen out of her love. Struck also by poverty and the financial crash, D. is heartbroken and freezes to death in his one room flat. D. imagines he is having a slow dance with J. as his imaginary partner and collapses on the stage, dying of pneumonia....

RED

BOOK

ROCK SONGS

Screamdream

When I get up and I go to bed
I hear these voices in my head

And I wake up screaming
And I wake up screaming
And I wake up screaming
And I wake up screaming for her

I had never been in love before
Until that day that I knocked on her door
Now I wake up screaming
I wake up dreaming
I wake up dreaming of her

I try to pretend that we are only friends But I don't think our
love can ever end I wake up dreaming
I wake up dreaming
I wake up dreaming of her

I met her in a bar, and she told me straight
That our future just wasn't that great
So, I wake up screaming
I wake up screaming
I wake up screaming
I wake up screaming for her

Stars

Stars shine, look down on the earth below
Greek gods, the spirits of the past
Lights reincarnated from ancient minds
Death could not kill the genii of our time

Stars observe the planets of their kingdom Life forms swarms
across the surface
Like ants working until they die

They cannot see their inner self and purpose
They watch what others do and think that they should follow
Copy others and achieve their own mediocrity

Leaders stand out in individual grandeur
The others look on and wonder at the greatness
The stars gleam now but once they were dim
Grief in the realisation of those around them

Temporary Friends

I've got temporary friends who pass me by from week to
week
They don't leave a trace unlike the tears that trickle down my
cheeks
(So many) different faces, none stay long, how can that be?
You think they're friends, but when it comes to it They're
only after one thing

CHORUS
Temporary friends
They'll get you in the end Temporary friends
Make friends break friends Temporary friends
They'll get you in the end
I had a good friend, but my mind is scarred with remembrance of
her
Visions flicker
Distorting in my view
She's imprinted in my brain, an indelible stain
Like a record skipping in the vein of my heart
The vein of my heart

Temporary friends
They'll get you in the end
Temporary friends
Make friends break friends
Temporary friends
They'll get you in the end

I've got temporary friends, who wave to me so they can jump the queue
Temporary friends, who promise to come round but never do
They seem to be devoid of any true emotion
They suck you in and spit you out

Temporary friends
They'll get you in the end
Temporary friends
Make friends break friends
Temporary friends and I can't keep waiting...

Special Keys

Took a good look in the mirror
Didn't like what I saw
Tried to change my shape
The thoughts in my mind

I watched my reflection flicker
A moment later it was still
A transformation took place
And the world was well

Escape from those barriers
You build around your ideals
Jump the fence
And run for home

Forget all your problems
They'll wait until tomorrow
Take your last drink
While you can

BLUES

Exam Blues

I revise for my exams, all on Saturday Night
It beats going out and getting into a fight
But I get so exhausted, I give up pretty soon
And I go up those stairs, up to my bedroom
I reach for my guitar and strum a few chords
And after twenty minutes I just get plain bored
I go into the bathroom and wash my hair
I've got teenage depression. Oh man it's not fair

When I go into the exam room, I'll forget all I know I'll be
sweating all over and then I'll want to go
I'm getting very nervous, my heart's all a flutter
I'm shaking all over, I don't know what's the matter I've got
the exam, got the exam, got the exam blues

Blues Injection

Pain is the focus and the power of my expression
I don't know where I'm going, I need some consolation
I've got a passion within me, but I'm devoid of direction
A screaming soul within me that is searching for perfection

Chorus 1:

The train is clicking along the track
But I'm strapped to the rails
There ain't no going back

My head is spinning with pain, my hand has lost its function
So now is the time to head for Heaven's Junction
You can pray to the Lord, there ain't no real compulsion
As Satan cries from every corner: 'Join my revolution!'

Chorus 2:

The train moves off but I'm caught in the Doors
And there ain't no real point in goin' back anymore

I had some nightmares, a kind of predilection
I went to work but they put me on a section
I went to the doctors, I thought I had an infection
But all they gave me was a Blues Injection

Chorus 3:

The pain went away just as the Doctor planned
Now I'm back playing the Blues
With my right hand

Manchester Blues

I've been to Manchester on the bus and the tram and the train
I've been to the Arndale Centre on the bus and the tram and the train But when I get home to Kearsley
It's time to go back again I've been to McDonalds And I've been to Pizzaland
I've been to the Piccadilly Chippy
And come out with a chip barm in my hand
And I've been to Burger King, but that don't mean anything
I've been down for so long
I don't think I'm ever coming back I've been so low for so long baby
I just can't seem to get back on track I've been to the Piccadilly 21 Club
And I've been to Royale's for a Royal with Cheese baby I've been to Sachas
And I've been to Principals I've been to Brahms & Liszt
But that doesn't rhyme with getting drunk Some people say I'm pretty hip
Others say I'm just a slime

Some people say I play the Blues too slow Others say it's out of time
But I'll go to Hell and back
Just to make my Blues Songs rhyme

LOVE SONGS

Jenna
Nov 1992

How can it be?
When I just met you
How can it be?
I hardly know you
That I'm… I'm in love with you
That I'm… I'm in love with you

And when I think
I think all day of you
And what's to come
I think I've thought it all through

And then one day
You'll have to go away
Or maybe then
If I plead with you to stay and say

That I'm... I'm in love with you
That I'm... I'm in love with you

I love your eyes
They are a cool jewelled blue
 I love your voice
I could listen to you...
Forever
I'm in love with you

Jenna
I want to marry you
And if you say, if you say I do
I'll be true to you

Princess   24.11.92

How can you tell if she's the one?
How do you know that your princess has come?
How can you trust that she'll wait for you?
How do you judge that her love is true?

A week of paradise out in the sun
Will it all last or will it soon be gone?
Will she believe that you meant what you said?
Will she come back once more and share your bed?

The wind of change whistles through the trees
Spring comes and Summer, Autumn leaves
You ask the question, your heart all a quiver
She offers her foot to fit the glass slipper

Chorus:It's because every time I see her
My heart goes round and round and
Every time she's away
I see her in my mind's eye
And I'm not alone any more

Jennifer   1992

It's real this time, it's not a dream
She's everything I want, everything I need

I don't want to change her not at all
Or rearrange the way she feels or cage her God forbid, cage her

Jennifer, here she comes with those sexy eyes
Here she comes dancing with all the guys
And here she comes, comes back to me

Oh Jennifer, here she comes and we're almost there
Here she comes, dancing with the sun in her hair
Here she comes, she's running back to me
And I know I want her And I know it's her

Only You   June 1993

I was born to write the songs
I was born to play guitar
I was born to kiss your hair
I was born before you were even there you were even there
 I was born to dance on stage
I was born a renegade
I was born to play the blues
I was born to be with you
I was born to walk with you
I was born to talk with you
I was born to help you through
I was born forever true to you
I was born to make your dreams come true
 I was born to see your eyes so blue
I was born to make love to you
I was born to marry you… to marry you
 And when you're here I'm alive
And when you're gone I'm nothing

Too Far Apart   June 1993

Oh! It's not you, it's me
I'm dreaming of things that can never be
Oh I don't wanna be without you
For the rest of my life
I can't stand to think of you and him
I want you to be my wife

Chorus:
But we're going nowhere
We're too far apart
How can we be together?
When we can never stay in each others' arms?

I stay at home, that's no good for me
When you're out with the boys, doing your thing
Can't you see you're hurting me?
Why do you say things to hurt me?

My Tulsa Queen   1993

Only 104
Only 104 days until I see her
Only a kiss away
Only a kiss away from falling in love

My Tulsa Queen
Where has she been
All of my life?
Now will you stay?
Oh come back and stay
Forever in my arms?

Only a flight away
Only a flight away
A flight of fancy

Only a long lost love
Only a long lost love
Born in ancient times

My Tulsa Queen
Are you just a dream?
Or are you real?

Now say you'll stay
Come back and stay
Forever in my arms

Only 24
Only 24 hours
From my dream girl

She is the one, She is the one

Everything &Nothing 9th August 1993

When I'm away from you
When I'm away from you I am nothing, I am nothing

When I am close to you
When I am close to you
I am everything, everything

Her heart is my heart
The heart is my heart
And it's on fire, and it's on fire
The diamond is a star
The diamond is a star
And it's on fire, it's on fire

I was dead before I saw you
Dead before you
Now I'm alive again, I'm alive again

Chorus 1:

Everything & Nothing
Worlds Apart
Everything & Nothing
Jewel in my heart

Chorus 2:
Everything & Nothing
Romancing the Stone
Everything & Nothing
Our love stands alone

A Story   *1993*

Barley white and fields of green
Tell me what it all means
The wind is raging through cherry trees
Blowing the gulls out to the seas

Garden of roses planted for two
Perfumed flowers of lavender blue
Spring came, then summer, autumn too
The cold winter went without you

I walked until I dropped in distant lands
Chopped and felled timber, red rough sore hands
I toiled all day and at night we planned
Our futures together, there's now just one man

She left the cabin he built in the woods
And she took the children all for their good
He never went out again, he never could
At night he slept, by day he chopped wood

He racked his brains and realized one day
He could enjoy his life, so he went away
Far around the world on the sea's blue haze
Meeting new people, on women he'd gaze

He'd seen the colours of suns which fall
He'd been to Berlin and seen the Wall
India & France, he smoked and drank gin
Until he realized true happiness came from within

The End of Love

A feeling
That's hard to pretend
An emotion
That all things transcends
And the void
The void when she goes
Love creeps up on you, then leaves you all alone

You miss her by day, you miss her by night
You try to forget, there is no respite
Can I say what I mean, can I say I love you?
Or will the door close once more, with you out of view?

A feeling
That's hard to explain
Like snow clouds that melt in the rain
And the void
The void when she goes
If she goes, heaven hell knows

Please don't cry, that sort of thing's for girls
But we're living in a liberated world
Can I say how I feel, can I say I love you?
Or will the door close once more, with you out of view?

Chorus 1:
When I'm with you, I laugh until dawn
Please don't ever leave me, now it's just begun
You may think I'm crazy, I'm going round the bend
But one thing I must say, I hope this song will never end

Chorus 2:
When I'm with you, I laugh until dawn
Please don't ever leave me, now it's just begun
You may think I'm crazy; I'm going round the bend
But one thing I must say, I hope this song is never going to
end

Never Say Never   *3.1.1994*

I'll never see her face again
I'll never fall in love again

Like I loved her
Like I loved her

I'll never see her face again
I wonder about her other men
I'll never be the same
I'll never be the same

I miss her, terribly
Never
How can it be?
Never say never

I'll never cross that bridge again
I'll never give myself again
Like I gave myself to her
I gave myself to her

I'll never trust a girl that way
I'll never speak of yesterdays
I'll never open up
I'll never open out

I can't forget her
Does she think of me?

Never say never
Never say never

Now She's Gone

When your world was one and the days were never long
She became a part of you
But now she's gone you miss sharing her feelings
And her thoughts and dreams
But is it that you miss sharing and giving all your love
Or are you still searching for a star in the sky above
You've got to realise you can't replace her
She's now a part of you
You've got to wait for someone who will come into your life
Sure and clear as the morning dew

Chorus:
I'm going to miss her for the rest of my life
But I've got to go on somehow
I'm going to miss her every time I hear her name
 Every time I see her face in my mind

Now she's gone Now she's gone
I am nothing

Now She's Gone (2)

In every day in every way she's my life
In every thought in every dream she's my life

And I can't begin to say what I'll do with my life
Now I can't begin to explain how I feel in my life

Now that she's gone

With every thought and every act I loved her
With every look and every touch I loved her

And I can't begin to say what I'll do with my life
No I can't begin to say what I'll do with my life
Now that she's gone

Oh come back
Baby come back
Into my arms

Cold Outside (Your Love)

It's cold outside
It's cold outside your love

Your Love has gone
Now it's time to carry on
With my life

Oh come back
Baby come back
Into my arms

Oh come back
Oh come back
Come back for ever
Come back forever
Forever

Now you can carry on with your life
Now you can concentrate your mind and soul
And it's alright

The sun will shine
In your eyes again

Slow Dance (Kiss Me in the Morning)

Verse 1:

Kiss me in the morning
And love me at night
I'll always watch out for you
Make sure I hold you tight

Chorus:
Because you are everything
And I've waited for all time
To make you mine

Verse 2

Be my friend forever
Let me be the one
Who picks you up when you fall down
I'll always be around

Chorus:
Because you are everything
And I've waited for all time
To make you mine

You are the first face I want to see in the morning
You are the first face I want to look at… at night
You are the last face I want to look at when it's over
And the last eyes at the end of the world

Sometimes You DoToo 1993

Sometimes when I'm alone at night
Sometimes when I'm alone
Well I get frightened
And I think you know that
Sometimes, you do too

And you can be all so alone
Even when you're with someone, it's not her
And you can be all so alone
You're with someone, she's not the one
You're thinking of
She's not the one
You're dreaming of
There will only be one
Who waits for you
Only be one
Who thinks of you
Only be one
Who's right for you

Sometimes when I'm alone at night
Nothing makes sense in the world
Without you
And I know you know
That you think so too

Nothing   12.9.1995

All the books are left unread
All the words they have been said
All the drinks they have been tasted
All our lives they have been wasted
We sat and watched the VCR
All got drunk in stinking bars
We all did nothing for our nation
What did we leave our next generation?

Chorus 1:Nothing, we left them nothing
Oh nothing, wasted for nothing
Nothing left behind
Nothing in our minds

Bridge 1:
If you could only see
You were meant for me
How much you meant to me
Everything & Nothing
We all write songs and make them rhyme
Playing suicide with father time

Everyone's playing the lottery
But if they win they won't be free

Alcohol and cigarettes, well they're all fine
They all mean nothing unless you're mine
Do a lot of work for charity
Maybe I'll win Saturday's, Saturday's Lottery

Chorus 2:
It all means nothing
Wasted for nothing, nothing
Nothing left behind
Nothing in our time

Bridge 2:
Although I dreamt of you
There was nothing I could do
You meant everything to me
Everything & Nothing
Everything & Nothing
Oo oo Oh &
Something & Anything

I Thought Of You 1995

I thought of you
I dreamt I never wanted
Any one but you
Any one but you

You came to me
On a night in cold November
It was cool to be
Cool to be

I held your waist
I kissed your lips
We swayed around and through the mist
I saw your eyes and I knew
You meant everything to me

And now you're gone
There's nothing to live for
Now you're with someone
Someone who isn't me

I chased you through
An Airport lounge in Paris
For a rendez-vous
For a rendez-vous

With the Blues…
Chicago Tenerife
We played around
And through the mist
I saw your eyes and I knew
You meant everything – Everything to me

BLUE BOOK

Cold Outside (your Love) Silver and Gold Version

It's cold outside, cold outside your love
Your Love has gone
Now it's time to carry on
With my life

Oh come back… baby come back…
Into my arms
Oh come back… Oh come back…
Come back for ever
Come back forever
Forever

Now you can carry on with your life
Now you can concentrate your mind and soul
And it's alright
The sun will shine
In your eyes again

The Same Old Slow Dance 1.6.2004

Verse 1:

Kiss me in the morning
And love me at night
I'll always watch out for you
Make sure I hold you tight

Chorus:

Because you're everything
And I've waited for all time
To make you mine

Verse 2:

Be my friend forever
Let me be the one
Who picks you up when you fall down
I'll always be around

Chorus:

Because you're everything
And I've waited for all time
To make you mine

You are the first face I want to see in the morning
You are the last face I want to look at… at night
You are the only face I want to see when it's over
The last eyes at the end of my world

Ooh… I love you… forever … I love you
Forever forever
forever forever
I love you
Forever

Chords:

The songs all have music composed for them which I know by heart and in some cases as I am so sure of the music I simply have not always written down all the chords in the songbook. Many recordings exist that I have copywritten and I hope soon to be able to produce music on manuscript paper in a forthcoming volume. All recordings and manuscript copies were copywritten and sent to my home address long ago by postal copyrighting methods. I am, however, providing chords for the following songs. All music copywritten 2009, rereleased on Tunecore and Ditto Music 2020.

RED BOOK

ROCK SONGS

Screamdream
Verses: Em A Em A then B to finish
Chorus: Em A … I wake up screaming

Stars

Verses: Em A Em A Em A Em A
Dm A Dm A Em A Em A

Temporary Friends

Verse: E D C A Chorus E F C# Bb

Special Keys

Verse: F# E D C# B E F# Chorus: AbB F# A AbB
F# A

BLUES

Exam Blues
Just blues.. Em A Em A B three chord thrash

Blues Injection

Verse 1: C C C C F F F F
Verse 2: C C C C F F C C
Chorus 1: G F C C
Chorus 2: G F C G
Chorus 3: G F C G

Manchester Blues

Em Am Em Am Em B A Em

LOVE SONGS
Jenna
A D A D G C

Princess
Verse: Em A Em A C Am C D
Chorus: G Em Am D G Em

Jennifer
Dm Cm Em Bm Dm Cm Em Bm #
(Chorus: A F#m F#m Bm E)
G Em

Too Far Apart
F Em Amaj F Em Amaj F E Amaj F Em Amaj
(Chorus: A Em A E D E)
 C Em Am D D C D C

My Tulsa Queen
Verse: Em B Dm A E Csus2 Em B Dm A E Csus2

Chorus: G#m F#m G#m F#m E Csus2 F#m Bb F#m BbD#

Everything & Nothing
B F#D B F#D B F#D B F#D F#E D E B A Ab
Chorus: Gm D Gm A B A B D D A G F# D A G F#
E F E D C#

A Story
D C Am Em F Em Amaj F Em

The End of Love
Em Csus2 Em Csus2 D F (without top E string) Em Csus2
Chorus: A G E

Never Say Never
Dm Dm Cm Cm Dm Dm Cm Cm Em F Amaj Dm Dm Cm Cm Dm Dm Cm Cm Amaj D Am C Em

Now She's Gone
A G C A G C Link: C A# C A# A Em
Chorus: A D A D E Bm

Now She's Gone (2)
G F G F C Bb C Bb Am A D C D C G F G F B E Bm
Bbm Fmaj

Cold Outside (Your Love)
Verse: G D# G D# A# G# A# G# Gm
Chorus: Am A# F E Bm F#m G Em Bm A Em A Em
G Bm G Bm Emaj

Slow Dance
Verse: D Am D Am F C Bb G
Chorus: C Bb Ab G (plus Bb)
Melody: D# D# C (+D#) D# D# C Ab Db Ab Db
Bridge + Instrumental Am Fm Em Fm Em Fm

Sometimes You Do Too
C# A#m C# A#m D# C#m D# C#m A#m
A# G# F# D# A# G# F# E C E C E B E B D G#

Nothing
Em Cmaj7 Em Cmaj7 Amaj Cmaj7 Amaj Cmaj7 Em
Cmaj7 Em Cmaj7 Amaj Cmaj7 Amaj Cmaj7 G F G F
Dm C# G F G Dm Dm A Em A Em A Em Cmaj7
Cmaj7

I Thought Of You
D D C C G G C F G G G F C Am F Cm

Cold Outside (your Love) Silver and Gold Version
Verse: G D# G D# A# G# A# G# Gm
Chorus: Am A# F E Bm F#m G Em Bm A Em A Em
G Bm G Bm Emaj

The Same Old Slow Dance
Verse: D Am D Am F C Bb G
Chorus: C Bb Ab G (plus Bb)
Melody: D# D# C (+D#) D# D# C Ab Db Ab Db
Bridge + Instrumental Am Fm Em Fm Em Fm

Manuscript Copies of the Red Book and the Blue

————————————

Book previously published in 2009.

1 From 'Norfolk' by John Betjeman.

2 Title of a song by ZZ Top

3 Title of a film Town Without Pity (1961), directed by Gottfried Reinhardt. With Kirk Douglas, Barbara Rütting, Christine Kaufmann. Gene Pitney sings 'Town without Pity' to accompany the film and the song was later covered by Ronnie Montrose.

4 Ironic play on the Beatles song 'Let it be'.

---

⁶ Born Free (1966) is a film directed by James H. Hill and produced by Sam Jaffe and Paul Radin with a musical score by John Barry. It commences with a song sung by Matt Munro, and stars Virginia McKenna and Bill Travers

5 La Vita è Bella (1997) is coincidentally the title of a film directed by Roberto Benigni, starring Roberto Benigni, Nicoletta Braschi and Giorgio Cantarini.

7 The opening words to 'Vincent' sung by Don Mclean are 'Starry, Starry night.'

8 'That whatsoever King may reign, I will be the Vicar of Bray, Sir!' are verses from the poem entitled 'The Vicar of Bray' in The British Musical Miscellany, Volume I, 1734. Text as found in R.
S. Crane, A Collection of English Poems 1660-1800. New York: Harper & Row, 1932.

9 Singin' in the Rain (1952) directed by Stanley Donen and Gene Kelly. With Gene Kelly, Donald O'Connor, Debbie Reynolds

10 My Fair Lady (1964), directed by George Cukor; with Audrey Hepburn, Rex Harrison, and Stanley Holloway.

www.ingramcontent.com/pod-product-compliance
Lightning Source LLC
Chambersburg PA
CBHW030530260626
4715TCB00005B/1957